Hannah's Way

Kar-Ben Publishing
A division of Lerner Publishing Group, Inc.
241 First Avenue North
Minneapolis, MN 55401 U.S.A.

Website address: www.karben.com

Library of Congress Cataloging-in-Publication Data

Glaser, Linda.
    Hannah's way / by Linda Glaser ; illustrations by Adam Gustavson.
      p.   cm.
    Summary: In rural Minnesota in 1932, Hannah, a young orthodox
Jewish girl, deals with being the new girl in class.
    ISBN 978-0-7613-5137-5 (lib. bdg. : alk. paper)
    [1. Moving, Household—Fiction. 2. Jews—United States—Fiction.
3. Schools—Fiction. 4. Minnesota—History—20th century—Fiction.]
I. Gustavson, Adam, ill. II. Title.
PZ7.G48047Han 2011
[E]—dc22   2009030919

PJ Library Edition 978-0-7613-9037-4

Manufactured in China
3-49193-12587-3/23/2020

102029.7K3/B0909/A7

Hannah's Way

Linda Glaser

illustrations by Adam Gustavson

KAR-BEN
PUBLISHING

"This Saturday is our autumn picnic," Miss Hartley reminded everyone.

Hannah's heart raced. The class picnic!
Maybe now she'd make some friends.

"We've reserved a spot at Grove Park," her teacher continued. "Let me know if you'll need someone to drive you."

Hannah's face fell. *Drive?* On *Saturday?*

Back home in Minneapolis, her friends would have understood. But here in northern Minnesota, no one would. No one else in the whole school was Jewish.

If only Papa hadn't lost his job, Hannah thought. If only Uncle Max hadn't asked him to come work in his general store way up here on the Iron Range. If only she weren't so far away from all her friends.

That night before bed, she told her parents about the picnic. "Please, may I go?"

"Hannah," said her mother, her eyes holding disapproval. "Ride in a car on Saturday?"

"Just this once?" Hannah begged.

Papa's voice was quiet but firm. "You know that Saturday is our day of rest. We don't work or drive on the Sabbath."

Hannah lay on her bed and sobbed. It was hard enough being new and having no friends. Now she would have to miss the class picnic, too.

The next day during spelling, Hannah looked around at her classmates. She knew only a few of them by name. Peter was a loudmouth. Sally always raised her hand with the right answers.

Ruth, who sat right next to Hannah, liked
to draw. Would any of them understand?

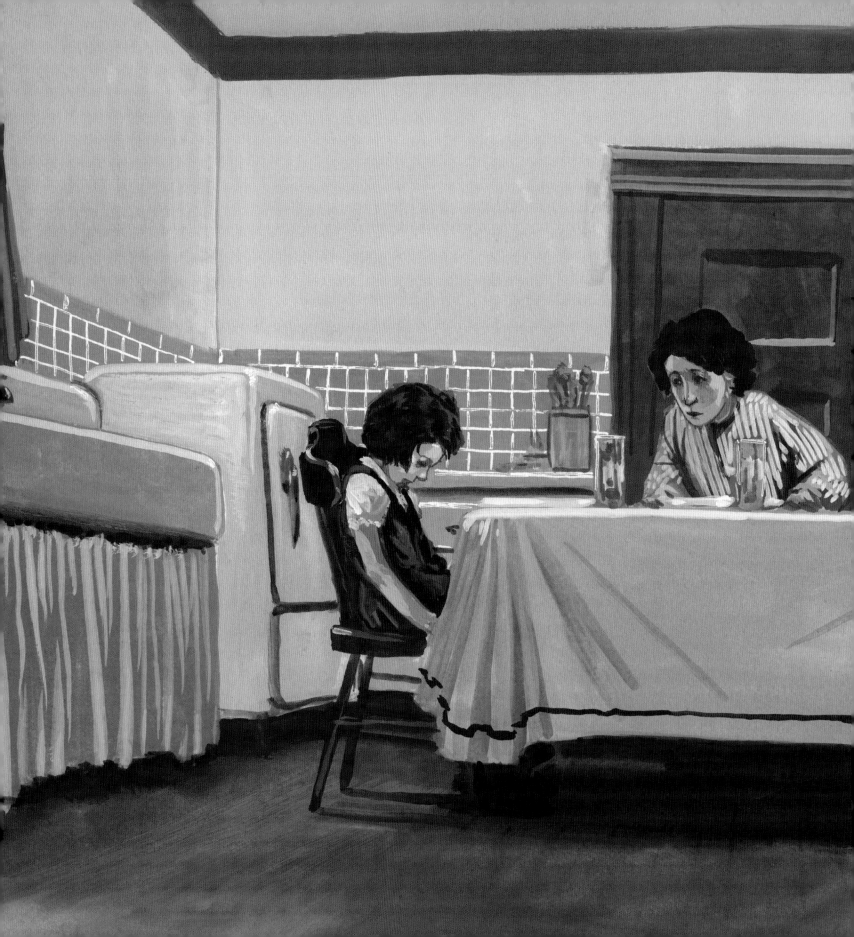

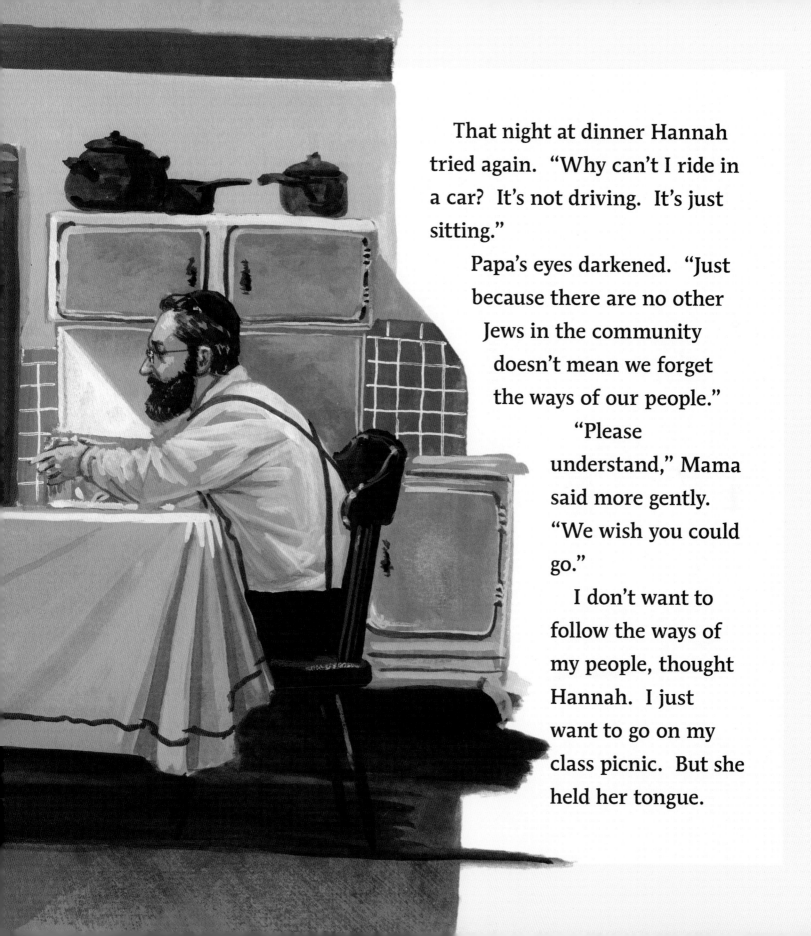

That night at dinner Hannah tried again. "Why can't I ride in a car? It's not driving. It's just sitting."

Papa's eyes darkened. "Just because there are no other Jews in the community doesn't mean we forget the ways of our people."

"Please understand," Mama said more gently. "We wish you could go."

I don't want to follow the ways of my people, thought Hannah. I just want to go on my class picnic. But she held her tongue.

On the playground the next day, everyone was making plans. Who would they go with? Who would they eat with? Hannah wanted to plug her ears.

"We have room in our car," Perfect Sally announced.

"Hannah!" Peter shouted across the playground. "Who are you going with?" Now everyone was watching her.

"I—I don't know yet." Hannah turned away.
Ruth was busy making a clover chain. She
looked up at Hannah and smiled as if she
might want to be friends. Hannah smiled
back hopefully.

When class was dismissed, Hannah hung behind. "Miss Hartley," she began in a small voice. "About the picnic... I—I want to go. But... about the car..." How could she explain? It would sound so strange.

"I understand." Miss Hartley smiled. "Don't worry. I'll find someone to drive you." She gave Hannah a reassuring pat on her head. "I'm glad you told me."

Hannah stood there a moment more, but no words would come.

All the way home, she kicked pebbles, thinking there must be a way to solve her dilemma. And suddenly it came to her.

"Mama, Papa," she burst in the door. "I'll *walk* to the park on Saturday!"

Mama shook her head. "It's two miles away. You can't go by yourself."

"What if someone goes with me?" Hannah pleaded.

Mama looked at Papa.

Papa nodded. "Now that's thinking."

Hannah felt like dancing! At least now she had a chance.

The next day, Hannah looked over at Ruth's drawing and smiled. "I like your horse."

"Thanks." Ruth smiled back.

Ask, Hannah told herself. Ask. But what if Ruth said, "You can't ride in a car on Saturday? How strange!" The whole day went by and still she couldn't ask.

The next day was Friday. It was her last chance, and Hannah had decided just what to say to Ruth. She had rehearsed it in her head: "I know this may sound silly..." But when the morning bell rang, Ruth's seat was empty.

When everyone else left for lunch, Hannah walked up to her teacher's desk. She took a deep breath. "Miss Hartley, about the picnic...." She searched for the right words.

"Oh, did I forget to tell you?" asked Miss Hartley. "You can go with Sally."

Hannah shook her head. This time she had to say it. "I'm—I'm not allowed," she blurted out. "Orthodox Jews don't ride in cars on Saturday." There, she'd said it. "But I can walk with someone. I just don't know who would want to walk with me."

Miss Hartley looked at Hannah kindly. "I'm glad you told me. Now let's see what we can do."

All during lunch Hannah wondered. Who will Miss Hartley ask? Probably Sally. Perfect Sally.

After lunch, Miss Hartley rang her bell. "Class, I've just learned that Hannah is not allowed to ride in a car on Saturdays. According to her Jewish faith, Saturday is the day of rest.

"But there may be a way for her to join us," Miss Hartley went on. "Hannah, please tell the class."

Hannah stared hard at her desk. "I—I can go if someone will walk with me," she whispered.

"Would someone do that?" asked Miss Hartley.

The class was silent. Hannah's heart pounded. No one will, she told herself. It's a crazy idea.

But then a desk creaked. Hannah lifted her head and looked.

Every hand was in the air!

Author's Note

The inspiration for this story came from a 1996 exhibit at the Minnesota History Center entitled *Unpacking on the Prairie: Jewish Women in the Upper Midwest*. One of the stories, about the only Jewish girl in a small town school, especially resonated with me. When she revealed to her teacher that as an Orthodox Jew she wasn't allowed to ride to a class picnic on Saturday, her classmates responded with a touching and unexpected kindness.

Like Uncle Max, some Eastern European Jewish immigrants moved to Minnesota's Iron Range in the late 19th and early 20th century to open general stores. They were often the only Jews in these small mining towns.

Other Jews, like Hannah's father, were born in Minneapolis to immigrant parents. Some lost their jobs during the Depression. In this story, Hannah's father was lucky to find new work in his brother's family business, even though it meant uprooting his family.

I wish to thank genealogist Joanne Sher for her help with historical accuracy.

Hilda, Charles, and Zelda Modelevsky at the Modelevsky family store in St. Paul, MN, in 1926. Everyone helped out in a family-owned business such as this one.

From the collections of the Jewish Historical Society of the Upper Midwest